MW01492180

BL 4.5
AR Pts 0.5

TOP 10 TOUGHEST FOOTBALL PLAYERS

BY JIM GIGLIOTTI

Published by The Child's World®
1980 Lookout Drive • Mankato, MN 56003-1705
800-599-READ • www.childsworld.com

Photo credits:
Adobe Stock: Pixelrobot (cover), 1; AP Photo: Morry
Gash 4, 17; David Durochik 6; Tony Tomsic 7, 9, 15;
Tom DiPace 10; Peter Read Miller 11; Rick Smith 12;
13; Greg Trott 19. Dreamstime.com: Danny Hooks 2.
Joe Robbins: 5, 8, 14, 16, 18. Shutterstock: Goir 20;
Larry St. Pierre 21.

ISBN: 9781503827295
LCCN: 2017960466

Printed in the United States of America
PA02380

50

CONTENTS

WHO'S NUMBER ONE?

At the end of a football game, everyone knows who won. It's the team with the most points! At the end of the NFL season, the No. 1 team is clear. It's the winner of the Super Bowl. Choosing the toughest NFL player of all time is a bit more difficult. Is it the guy who plays the most games? Or the player who delivers the hardest hits? Is it a quarterback who never leaves the lineup? Or a running back who carries the ball all the time? Fans, experts, and fellow players all have their opinions.

Opinions are different than facts. Facts are real things. Brett Favre started more games in a row than any other quarterback in NFL history. That's a fact. Ronnie Lott was the most punishing tackler ever. That's an opinion. A football field is 100 yards long. That's a fact.

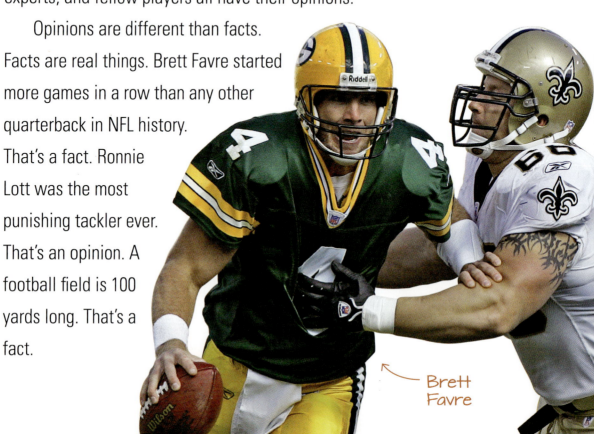

Brett Favre

Lambeau Field is the best place to watch a football game. That's an opinion. Some people might think Mike Singletary was a harder hitter than Ronnie Lott. That's fine; that's their opinion. But they can't say Lott didn't play for four Super Bowl-winning teams in San Francisco. That's a fact. Packers fans think Lambeau is No. 1. But you would find a very different opinion in lots of other NFL stadiums, where fans think THEIR place is No. 1.

And that's where *you* come in. You get to choose who is the toughest player in NFL history. You will read lots of facts and stories about these great players. Based on that, what's your opinion? There are no wrong answers about who is the toughest NFL player of all time . . . but you might have some fun discussions with your football-loving pals!

Read on and then after you're done, make up your own Top 10 list.

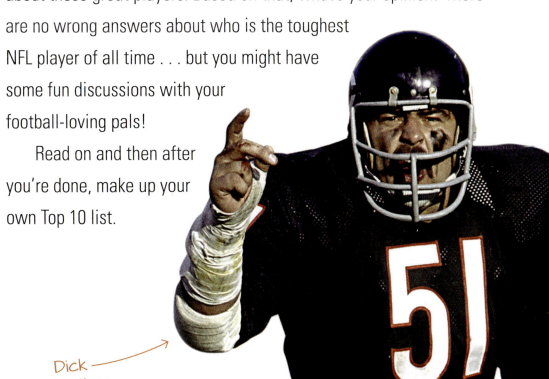

Dick Butkus

EARL CAMPBELL

HOUSTON OILERS • NEW ORLEANS SAINTS

Words help, but they're not enough. You need video. There's Earl Campbell head-butting a Rams **linebacker**. He knocked the guy flat on his back before heading downfield. There's Campbell taking a ferocious hit at the goal line. The Raiders defensive back thought he had stopped Campbell cold. He didn't. Campbell bounced off and twisted into the end zone! Campbell's best weapons were his powerful legs. Sportscaster Rich Eisen once called them "basically two tree trunks with cleats at the bottom." Those legs kept him churning for more yardage, even after contact with a defender. Campbell's fierce determination also played a big part in making him one of the toughest men ever with the football in his hand.

Campbell led the NFL in rushing each of his first three seasons in the league.

NUMBERS, NUMBERS

Campbell was only 5 feet 11 inches tall, but weighed 232 pounds. He was very busy. He carried the ball nearly 22 times per game during his six-plus seasons with the Oilers.

MEAN JOE GREENE

PITTSBURGH STEELERS

Greene recovered 16 fumbles in his 13-year career. He was also named to 10 Pro Bowls.

Mean Joe Greene isn't really mean. Instead, the Hall of Fame defensive end's nickname came from the nickname of his college, North Texas State University. The school's sports teams are known as the "Mean Green."

Offensive linemen who had to block Mean Joe found that his nickname fit just right. Greene had size and speed and great moves. He was the 1969 Defensive Rookie of the Year. Then he was a key part of Pittsburgh's "Steel Curtain" defense. Mean Joe helped the Steelers win the Super Bowl four times in the 1970s. He also was named the NFL Defensive Player of the Year in 1972 and 1974.

Greene made a famous Super Bowl TV ad. In it, a boy shares his soft drink with the tough-guy football player. Mean Joe then gruffly walks away. But he stops, turns, and throws the kid his jersey. See, he was not so mean after all.

NUMBERS, NUMBERS

Greene wore uniform No. 75 during his NFL career. It is one of only two numbers ever officially retired—meaning that no other player will ever wear it—by the Steelers.

DEACON JONES

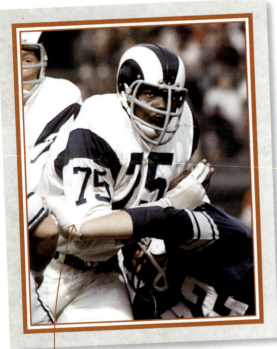

Jones's real first name was David. He called himself Deacon because, he figured, "Nobody would ever remember a player named David Jones!"

NUMBERS, NUMBERS

The NFL record for sacks in a season is 22.5, by Michael Strahan of the New York Giants in 2001. But that's only because sacks were not an official league stat in Deacon's time. Unofficially, he had 26 sacks in 14 games in 1967.

Deacon Jones is credited with inventing the **sack**. He wasn't the first player ever to tackle a passer behind the line of scrimmage. He was the first player to *call* it a sack. Why that word? He said it was like "the devastation of a city." Another word for that is . . . sack!

Jones was a defensive end. He played on the Los Angeles Rams "Fearsome Foursome" line of the 1960s and early 1970s. He probably was one of the fastest defensive linemen ever. He was one of the most physical, too. He tried to burst past his blockers. Sometimes, he might give one a whack on the side of the helmet. That was his' famous "head slap."

The head slap is a penalty now, but "you haven't lived until you've had your bell rung by Deacon a few times," one opponent said.

RAY NITSCHKE

GREEN BAY PACKERS

Off the field, Ray Nitschke wore glasses and was a very quiet fellow. You might think he was a librarian! On the field, the Packers linebacker was one of the toughest players ever to play the game.

Once he stepped between the lines, he would do whatever it took to get to the ball carrier. He would grab, hit, or throw an elbow. And that was just during practice! You can't do that inside a library!

Ball carriers feared this hard hitter. Quarterbacks ran away from him. Blockers knew they would need help to stop him. Even his fierce look scared some players! Nitschke's favorite move was to smack his forearm across a ball carrier's chest. He knew that gave him an advantage. "You want the ball carrier to be a little shy," he said, "and a little shyer the next time."

Nitschke was voted into the Pro Football Hall of Fame on his first try in 1978.

NUMBERS, NUMBERS

Five: That's the number of NFL championships the Packers won in the 1960s with Nitschke anchoring the middle of the club's defense.

MIKE SINGLETARY

CHICAGO BEARS

Ever see a cartoon where the eyes pop out of a character's head? That's what Mike Singletary looked like before every play began.

Singletary was one of the most intense players ever to strap on a helmet. Nothing escaped his notice before the play started. His eyes darted back and forth, taking it all in. When the ball was snapped, he knew exactly where to go—after the ball! More often than not, he met the runner at the line. He laid on a crunching hit that sent the opponent to the ground.

The toughest players don't walk around telling everyone how tough they are. Everybody just knows it. In this great linebacker's case, opponents and fans knew it just by looking at his eyes.

NUMBERS, NUMBERS

Over his last 11 NFL seasons, Singletary played in 163 regular-season games for the Bears. He started at middle linebacker in every one of them.

Singletary was the NFL Defensive Player of the Year for 1985. That season, the Bears won the Super Bowl.

JACK YOUNGBLOOD

LOS ANGELES RAMS

Defensive end Jack Youngblood once played in a Super Bowl on a broken leg. That is not a typo. That is *tough*!

In a 1979 playoff game, the Rams met the Dallas Cowboys. An opponent rolled into Youngblood's leg. It broke just above his ankle. "Tape it up!" Youngblood yelled. He returned to the field!

The Rams weren't expected to beat Dallas, but they did. That earned them a spot in the NFC Championship Game the next week at Tampa Bay. Youngblood wasn't expected to play because of his leg, but he did. The Rams beat the Buccaneers, and Youngblood started in Super Bowl XIV against Pittsburgh.

It was nothing new. The Rams captain missed only one game in his 14-year career.

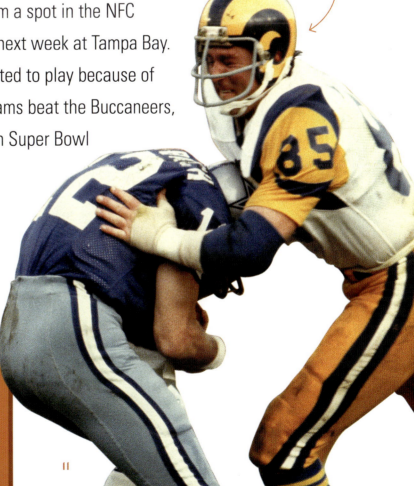

Youngblood's jersey included his first name. Why? Jim Youngblood also played for the Rams. The two players were not related!

NUMBERS, NUMBERS

Unofficially, Youngblood had 151.5 sacks in his 202 career games. Sacks were not an official NFL statistic until 1982.

CHUCK BEDNARIK

PHILADELPHIA EAGLES

You know a player was tough if one of his nicknames was "Concrete Charlie!" Another nickname for Chuck Bednarik was "The Sixty-Minute Man." He earned it by taking part in every play on offense and defense. He played all 60 minutes when the Eagles beat the Green Bay Packers in the 1960 NFL Championship Game. In the NFL's early days, many players played "both ways." By 1960, Bednarik was the only one.

In the 1960 NFL Championship Game, Bednarik lined up at **center** when the Eagles had the ball. He played linebacker for the Eagles' D. He made the play of the game, too. The Packers had a chance to pull out the victory in the final seconds. Bednarik tackled star running back Jim Taylor in the open field to prevent a touchdown. Then he wouldn't let Taylor get up! The clock ran out, the game ended, and the Eagles were champions.

This is how Bednarik's hands looked after his long football career.

One of the most famous photos in NFL history is of Bednarik. He is standing over New York Giants star Frank Gifford. Gifford had been laid out flat by a crushing hit from Concrete Charlie. Bednarik later said he regretted the photo because the hit put Gifford on the sideline for a season. Still, it was a perfect example of how tough Bednarik was—and how tough a game football is.

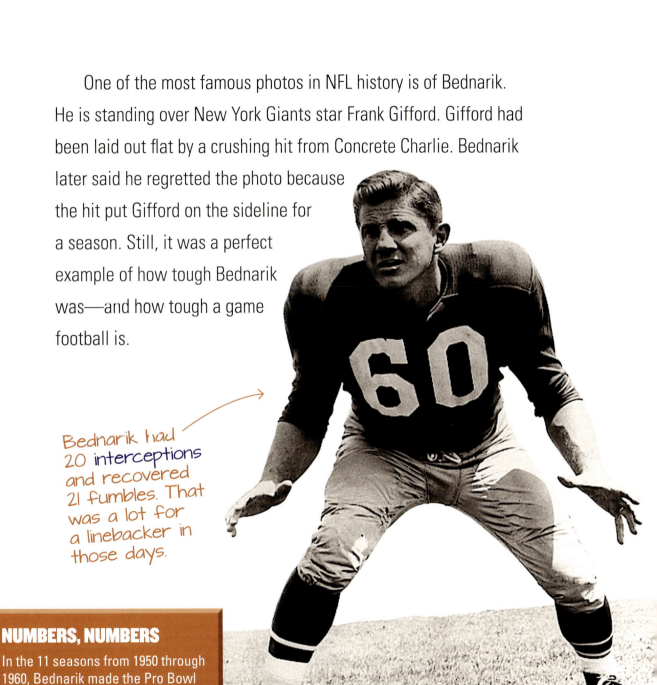

Bednarik had 20 interceptions and recovered 21 fumbles. That was a lot for a linebacker in those days.

DICK BUTKUS

CHICAGO BEARS

One day in the 1960s, the Baltimore Colts were on their team bus on the way to the airport. They had just played a game in Chicago against the Bears. A car smacked into the back of the bus. It shook and bounced! "Butkus!" the Colts players all said. Huh?

Being hit by Dick Butkus was like getting hit by a car. The great linebacker played only nine seasons. Still, his bone-rattling hits on opposing quarterbacks and ball carriers became legendary.

The Bears had many hard-nosed players like Butkus. They got a famous nickname: "The Monsters of the Midway!"

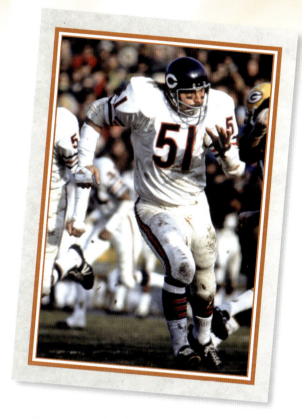

"I wanted to put someone on his back every time I lined up," Butkus said. "I guess I started to get a reputation."

That reputation was as one of the fiercest players in NFL history. As tough as he was, he was also great in pass coverage.

He intercepted 22 passes in his career, still among the best by a Bears player. He also recovered 27 fumbles. That's one of the top marks in NFL history. And he did all that even though he had first injured his knees in high school.

Butkus's knees got very bad late in his career. He couldn't even practice during the week. He'd play on Sunday, then rest his aching knees for six days. Once Sunday rolled around, he was back on the field. Nothing was going to keep this tough guy out of the lineup.

NUMBERS, NUMBERS

Eight: That's the number of times Butkus made the Pro Bowl in his nine seasons in the NFL. He was an All-Star every season except his last.

BRETT FAVRE

ATLANTA FALCONS • GREEN BAY PACKERS
NEW YORK JETS • MINNESOTA VIKINGS

From 1992 to 2007, Brett Favre started every game at quarterback for the Green Bay Packers. In that same time, the Atlanta Falcons started 16 different quarterbacks. P.S.: The Falcons traded Favre after the 1991 season. You can be sure they wish they hadn't!

Favre ended his career in 2010 with the Vikings. When he retired, he was the NFL's all-time leader with 71,838 yards and 508 touchdowns passing. His streak of never missing a start ended at 297 games. That's an impressive **ironman** streak.

It's true that quarterbacks don't get hit on every play. But when they do get hit, it's often brutal. They might not see it coming. A defensive lineman can smack them on their **blind side**. Or, they see it coming from a pass rusher with a full head of steam.

Favre led his teams to 199 wins, third most ever for a quarterback.

Still, the QB stands in to finish the throw. The hit is the price they pay. You've got to be tough to hang in there like that!

Playing QB takes mental toughness, too. He is the only player who needs to know exactly what all the other players are doing.

You've got to be incredibly tough to start every game in a single season . . . let alone in 17 seasons in a row, like Favre did.

He was pretty good in those games, too. He led the Packers to a win in Super Bowl XXXI. The Packers made the playoffs 10 times under Favre. He also took the Vikings there once. Think QBs are soft? Not this guy.

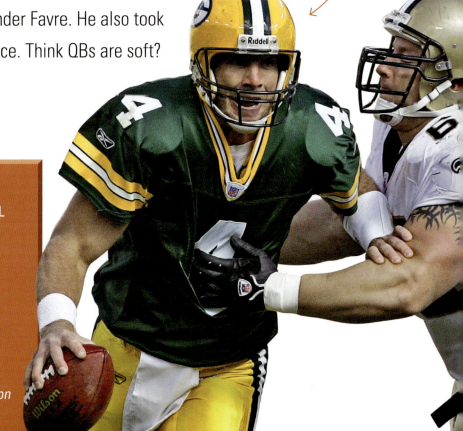

NUMBERS, NUMBERS

Most Consecutive Starts by an NFL Quarterback

(Regular-season games)

1. Brett Favre	297
2. Eli Manning	210
3. Peyton Manning	208
4. Philip Rivers	*192
5. Matt Ryan	*131

*active streak at end of 2017 season

RONNIE LOTT

SAN FRANCISCO 49ERS
LOS ANGELES RAIDERS • NEW YORK JETS

Here's all you need to know about how tough Ronnie Lott is. He once hurt his pinky. He would have had to miss a few games while it got better. Instead, he had another solution. Cut it off, he told the doctors. Yow! And, actually, the doctors snipped off a piece of his finger. Lott didn't miss a game.

There's more. He was one of the hardest-hitting defensive backs in pro football history. Said famous coach Pete Carroll, "Nobody's ever tried to hit a guy harder than Lott does." Legendary Dallas Cowboys coach Tom Landry said Lott hit like a middle linebacker from his position in the **secondary**.

Lott was the San Francisco 49ers' first-round draft pick in 1981. He made an immediate impact.

He was a starter as a rookie and intercepted seven passes. He ran three of them back for touchdowns. He brought a swagger and intensity to the team. The 49ers had been bad before his arrival. They had won a total of 10 games in the previous three seasons.

With Lott leading the defense, the Niners were not pushed around anymore. San Francisco won the Super Bowl his first year. Then they added three more titles in his 10 seasons with the club.

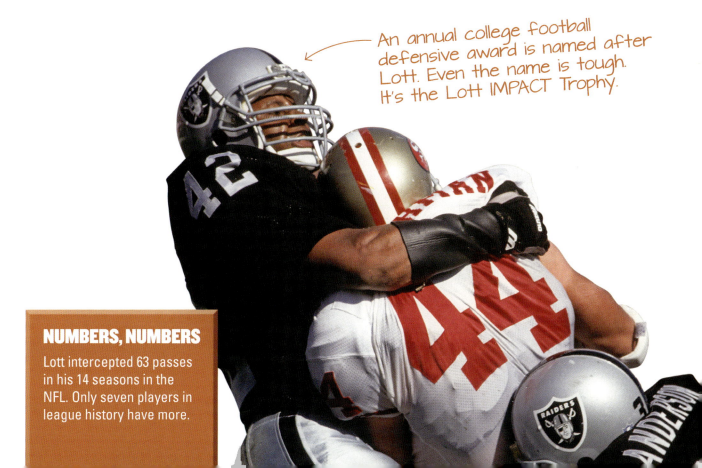

An annual college football defensive award is named after Lott. Even the name is tough. It's the Lott IMPACT Trophy.

NUMBERS, NUMBERS

Lott intercepted 63 passes in his 14 seasons in the NFL. Only seven players in league history have more.

YOUR TOP TEN!

In this book, we listed our Top 10 toughest football players. We gave you some facts and information about each player. Now it's your turn to put the players in order. Find a pen and paper. Now make your own list! Who is the No. 1 toughest football player of all-time? How about your other nine choices? Would they be the same players as we chose? Would they be in the same order? Are any players missing from this book? Who would you include? Put them in order—it's your call!

Remember, there are no wrong answers. Every fan might have different choices in a different order. Every fan should be able to back up their choices, though. If you need more information, go online and learn. Or find other books about these great players. Then discuss the choices with your friends!

THINK ABOUT THIS...

Here are some things to think about when making your own Top 10 list:

• What position did he play?

• What did his teammates and opponents think about him?

• Did the player help his team win?

• What made him such a tough player?

SPORTS GLOSSARY

blind side (BLYND SYDE) the direction the quarterback's back faces when he sets up to throw

center (SENN-ter) offensive lineman who starts each play by snapping the ball to the quarterback

fumble (FUMM-bull) a ball that is dropped by the player carrying it

interception (in-ter-SEPP-shun) a pass that is caught by the defense

ironman (EYE-ern-man) slang for a player who rarely or never comes out of a game

linebacker (LINE-bak-er) a defensive position that sets up behind the defense line

offensive linemen (aw-FENCE-uv LINE-men) players who protect the quarterback and block for running plays

sack (SAK) a play on which the quarterback is tackled behind the line of scrimmage, where the play started

secondary (SEK-un-dare-ee) a group name for the cornerbacks and safeties on defense who defend against pass plays

FIND OUT MORE

IN THE LIBRARY

Buckley, James Jr., and Jim Gigliotti. *Football: The Ultimate Insiders' Guide.* Santa Barbara, CA: Beach Ball Books, 2018.

The Editors of Sports Illustrated Kids. *Big Book of WHO Football* (Revised and Updated). New York: Sports Illustrated Kids, 2015.

ON THE WEB

Visit our Web site for links about Top 10 toughest football players: **childsworld.com/links**

Note to Parents, Teachers, and Librarians: We routinely verify our Web links to make sure they are safe and active sites. So encourage your readers to check them out!

INDEX

ABOUT THE AUTHOR

Jim Gigliotti is a former editor at the National Football League who is now an author. He has written more than 80 books on a variety of topics for adults and young readers, including several biographies in the popular "Who Was?" series for children.